T2-BP

D0478431

XX HAV

Havill, Juanita.

The magic fort

SOUTH ONTARIO BRANCH LIBRARY

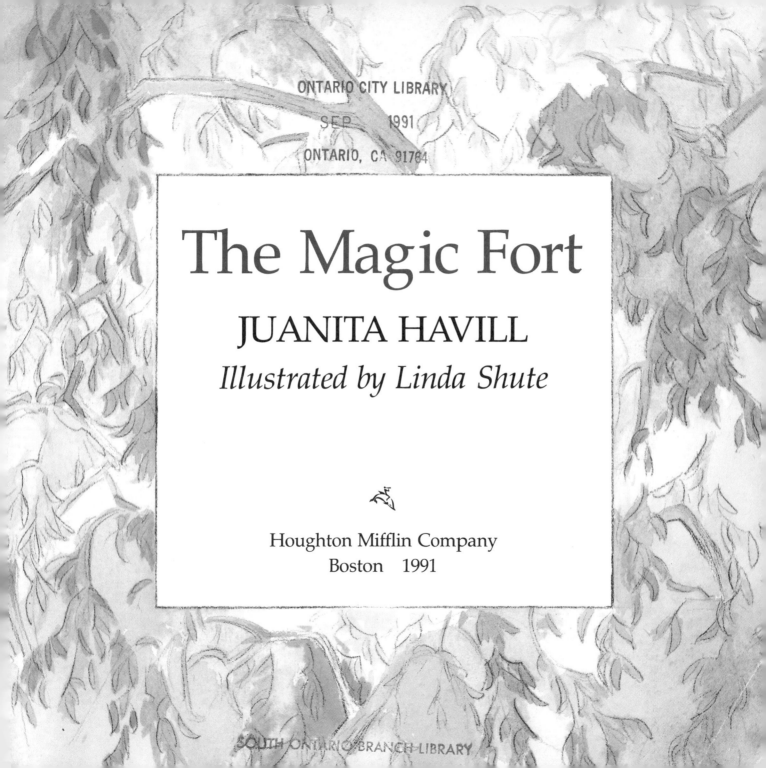

ONTARIO CITY LIBRARY

SEP   1991

ONTARIO, CA 91764

The Magic Fort

JUANITA HAVILL

Illustrated by Linda Shute

Houghton Mifflin Company
Boston   1991

SOUTH ONTARIO BRANCH LIBRARY

For the Solsengs, especially John, and for Gustav

— J. H.

Library of Congress Cataloging-in-Publication Data
Havill, Juanita.
  The magic fort / Juanita Havill ; illustrated by Linda Shute.
    p.   cm.
  Summary: While playing in their "magic fort," an easily climbable
tree, Kevin's brother Joseph breaks his arm, teaching both boys a
lesson in responsibility and playing together.
  ISBN 0-395-50067-2
  [1. Brothers — Fiction.   2. Trees — Fiction.]   I. Shute, Linda,
ill.   II. Title.
PZ7.H31115Mag   1991   90-42012
[E] — dc20   CIP
                            AC

Text copyright © 1991 by Juanita Havill
Illustrations copyright © 1991 by Linda Shute

All rights reserved. For information about permission
to reproduce selections from this book, write to
Permissions, Houghton Mifflin Company, 2 Park Street,
Boston, Massachusetts 02108.

Printed in the United States of America
WOZ 10   9   8   7   6   5   4   3   2   1

The Magic Fort

"Bye, Mom. I'm going to the magic fort," Kevin said.
The screen door banged shut behind him. Then it opened
and banged again.

"Can I come too?" Joseph asked.

"No," said Kevin. He didn't want to share the magic fort with his little brother. The fort was a big willow tree with branches that hung down all around. Kevin could be a soldier in a tent. Or he could climb up and be a pirate. Or he could explore the planets in a spaceship. Joseph was too young to climb.

"Kevin," Mom said, "you let Joseph go with you. He doesn't have any friends to play with right now, and you don't either."

"But I'm going to the magic fort."

"Joseph can go too. Just don't let him climb the tree."

"Oh, all right," Kevin said.

Joseph ran to Kevin and smiled. "Let's go," he said.

Kevin walked so fast that Joseph had to trot to keep up.

The curving branches of the weeping willow shook like curtains in the breeze. Kevin stepped into the fort and sat down against the tree trunk.

"Where's the magic?" Joseph said. "Ke-vin, where's the magic?"

Kevin stood up. He grabbed a branch and pulled himself up. "You have to make your own magic," he said.

"How?" asked Joseph.

"You just do," Kevin said. "Don't ask so many questions."

He pulled himself up to the next branch. Up and up he climbed, until he could see large patches of blue sky.

"Help me climb up, Kevin. I want to climb up too."

Kevin had never been up so high. He sat in the highest crow's-nest of his pirate ship and scanned the ocean. He felt tall and strong as he watched Joseph jump under a branch.

Joseph caught the branch and pushed his feet against it. Then he heaved himself up. Kevin couldn't believe it. Kevin couldn't climb like that when *he* was four.

Then Joseph stood on the branch and hopped to grab
the one above him. He hung from the branch.
"My hands are slippery. Help, Kevin!" Joseph shouted.

Before Kevin could move, Joseph slipped. His legs hit
the branches and he landed on his side on the ground.
He started crying. "My arm hurts," he screamed.

Kevin climbed down so fast that he scratched his hands and bumped his head. He held Joseph gently and helped him up. He could feel his brother's shoulders shaking. He wanted Joseph to be all right.

When they got home, Kevin told Mom what had happened.

"Kevin, I told you to watch Joseph," she said. "I told you he's too little to climb trees."

Mom put an ice bag on Joseph's arm. She washed Joseph's face. Then she called Dad and the doctor.

"Kevin, I have to take Joseph to the clinic. Dad will be home in a few minutes to stay with you."

Kevin wanted to hear Mom say that everything would be all right, but she left in a hurry.

Dad fixed supper, but Kevin wasn't hungry. He didn't even want to play catch after supper.

"Do you want to show me what happened?" Dad said.

Kevin stood under the lowest branch of the magic fort and showed Dad everything — except he jumped from the branch instead of falling.

"You shouldn't climb up high when Joseph is around," Dad said. "He always wants to do what you do, even if he's too little."

"I know," Kevin said. "Will Joseph be all right?"

"I think so," Dad said. "But he had quite a tumble."

Dad started walking back to the house. Kevin
stood alone in the fort. It was still and empty.
The magic was gone.

It was late when Joseph and Mom came home. Kevin came out to the living room to see him.

Joseph's arm was in a cast. He looked tired, but he smiled. "It's broken," he said. "They took a picture of my arm. You can write on my cast tomorrow. It's too wet now."

Kevin touched the cast carefully. "Does it hurt?"

"A little," said Joseph. "Are you mad at me?"

"No."

"Will you take me to the magic fort again?" Joseph asked.

Kevin remembered how empty the fort had been that night. "Yes," he said, "when you are better. But we have to make our magic on the ground, not up in the branches."

Mom put Joseph to bed. Then she came into Kevin's room. She hugged him and said, "Everything's going to be all right."